This book belongs

.... Florie & Jem ....

Happy reading!
Ray Abury

For my granddaughter, Emelia, who loves dinosaurs.

First published 2020 by Amazon UK.

This 2nd edition published 2021 by Amazon UK.

Copyright © Roy P. Awbery 2021

All rights reserved.

ISBN: 9798565257175

Some dinosaurs were big.

Some dinosaurs were small.

But mouse wanted to know

Who was the scariest of them all?

The Scariest Dinosaur

Some were big; some were small, and mouse wondered aloud,

'Who is the scariest of them all?'

Stegosaurus grunted, 'Of course, with my armour plates and sharp tail, it must be me.'

And he swished his spikey tail and got it stuck in a tree!

Brontosaurus laughed. 'No, the scariest is me, without a doubt.'

'I am the biggest and loudest, just hear me shout!'

'But,' said Pterodactyl, 'you look like an overgrown cow. Eating plants and leaves makes you scary how?'

'No, if the scariest is what you seek then it is me with my giant wings and razor-sharp beak.'

'But,' said Triceratops, 'you look like an over-sized bat! You are about as scary as a pussy cat!'

'No, the scariest dinosaurs have horns, so it is me, and the scariest have not one, or two, but three!'

'But,' said a Camposaurus, 'you are heavy and slow and your horns can crack.'

'No, the scariest dinosaurs do not need horns if they hunt as a pack.'

'But,' said Velociraptor, 'you are no bigger than chickens and have tiny jaws.'

'No, the scariest dinosaur is me with my sharp teeth and razor-like claws.'

'But,' said T-Rex, 'you are just half the size of me and with my big jaws I could eat you for my tea!'

'No, the scariest dinosaur is, without a doubt, me.'

'My sharp teeth and bellowing roar make everyone flee.'

And sure enough, no sooner had T-Rex said, all the others quickly fled.

'Well, I didn't run,' said the mouse with some zest.

'So you cannot be the scariest, or I would have left with the rest.'

'In fact,' continued mouse, 'I think I might be scarier than you!'

T-Rex laughed out loud and said,
'Mouse, you really haven't a clue!'

Suddenly, out of nowhere, a stampeding herd of mammoths came into sight.

T-Rex took one look and instantly fled in fright.

To the first mammoth mouse said, 'I guess you must be the scariest of them all.'

But at first the mammoth did not see the mouse because he was so small.

And as the mammoth looked for the voice unseen...

He gazed down, saw the mouse and...let out a scream!

You see, although mammoths are the size of a house, they are totally terrified of a miniscule mouse!

The mammoths ran with all their speed, frightfully fearful of a mouse indeed.

The mouse looked around and thinking he was alone, said with glee, 'So, the scariest creature here is me!'

The Author

Roy P. Awbery started off telling stories to his children and then began writing them for his three grandchildren. This is the first book he has published with many more to follow. Roy is also a scientist (his day job!) and a successful artist with his paintings furnishing homes and offices around the globe and has been featured on BBC radio. Roy lives in Berkshire, England with his wife, cat and two dogs, Jess and Ruby.

The illustrations in this book, and many more paintings, can be purchased at www.awberyart.com

A colouring book also accompanies this story book and is available on Amazon.

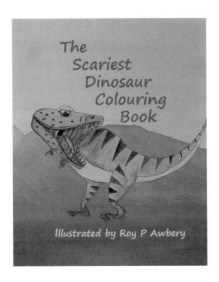

Coming soon: 'I Saw a Dinosaur' a fun illustrated story book with yet more dinosaurs and lots more creatures to try to find.

Follow me on Instagram @awberyart

Printed in Great Britain
by Amazon